good deed rain

49 Books by Allen Frost

...Ohio Trio...Bowl of Water...
...Another Life...Home Recordings...
...The Mermaid Translation...The Selected
Correspondence of Kenneth Patchen...
...The Wonderful Stupid Man...
...Saint Lemonade...Playground...Roosevelt...
...5 Novels...The Sylvan Moore Show...
...Town in a Cloud...A Flutter of Birds
Passing Through Heaven: A Tribute to Robert
Sund.......At the Edge of America.......
....Lake Erie Submarine....The Book of Ticks....
.........I Can Only Imagine.........
...The Orphanage of Abandoned Teenagers...
...Different Planet...Go With the Flow: A
Tribute to Clyde Sanborn...Homeless Sutra...
..The Lake Walker..A Hundred Dreams Ago..
....Almost Animals....The Robotic Age....
....Kennedy....Fable....Elbows & Knees:
Essays and Plays....The Last Paper Stars....
...Walt Amherst is Awake...When You Smile
You Let in Light....Pinocchio in America....
....Florida....Blue Anthem Wailing....
...The Welfare Office...Island Air...
...Imaginary Someone...Violet of the Silent
Movies....The Tin Can Telephone....
....Heaven Crayon....Old Salt....
...A Field of Cabbages...River Road...
....The Puttering Marvel....
..Something Bright...The Trillium Witch...
...Cosmonaut...Thriftstore Madonna...

THRIFTSTORE
MADONNA

THRIFTSTORE MADONNA ©2021
Allen Frost, Good Deed Rain
Bellingham, Washington
ISBN 978-1-0879-8001-0

Writing: Allen Frost
Cover Art: From a thriftstore somewhere
Interior Drawings: Allen Frost
Cover Production: Fred Sodt
Apple: TFK!
Author Photo on back cover: Larry Smith

Movie Quote Credits:
The Invisible Man vs. The Human Fly, Daiei Film, 1957.
Our Relations, Hal Roach Studios, 1937.

"Invisibility is no longer in the realm of impossibility."
—Professor Hayakawa

THRIFTSTORE MADONNA

Allen Frost

Good Deed Rain ◊ Bellingham, Washington ◊ 2021

the CHAPTERS

"You've got to be right once in your life."

—Oliver Hardy

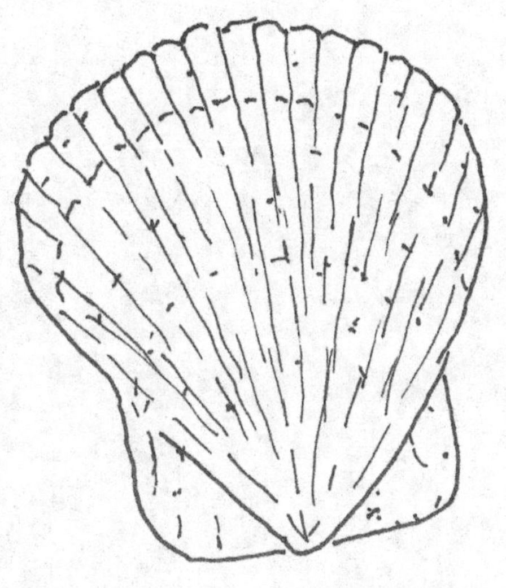

The MOVIE SHE IS IN

Tugboat Annie exists in a black and white fog. It clouds from the smokestack and wraps her like cotton. Steering the choppy ocean, she keeps one hand on the wheel and draws a long shrill note from the whistle. As if by magic, words are painted over her: STARRING MARIE DRESSLER.

The TUBA of SAINT MARK'S CATHEDRAL
pt. 1

During the Blitz, the Murphy family lived underground most of the time. They were cramped in that burrow for the duration, listening to bombs and rockets crunch above. Then of all the times, their daughter decided to learn the tuba. There was no school anymore, they were cooped up below London with nothing else to do. They tried to delicately explain how she really didn't need to play tuba, there were other, calmer things to master like Spanish guitar. But her mind was made up and every day the tin ration cans on the shelf would rattle. Her family found ways of being discreet with scarves wrapped over their ears until they just had to ask her to give them a little peace. It was a war and they couldn't even hear the bombs!

The TUBA of SAINT MARK'S CATHEDRAL pt. 2

They led her upstairs, out the latched door into what used to be a backyard full of flowers. Not anymore. Her mother placed a chair in the rubble and said, "You can play your tuba here for all the world to hear." Then her family crept back underground quickly. She sat down and the chair creaked. The tuba was the brightest thing on the landscape, a brass dandelion. One that sounded like the two o'clock train bound for Brixton before it was blown off the tracks. The music she played clawed at the air and held on for dear life like all the balloons of prayers that float from a cathedral.

The SQUIRRELS' BUTLER

Ordinarily you wouldn't expect to find a butler standing next to a redwood tree. Tuxedo, sunshine, black dress shoes on a bed of needles. He kept guard beside a long string that led up two hundred feet of red bark. Like a studio apartment in the clouds, they lived in luxury. The sound of the little silver bell meant they wanted him; they were ready to start the day.

The BERNARD MALAMUD BOUNCE

I said something I regret about Bernard Malamud. I had no right to say it, I can only hope he will forgive me and let me make it up somehow. It took all morning to think of a way. My dog and I were in the field when I threw the ball for her, announcing, "This one's for Bernard Malamud!" and off it went. An apology chased by a dog running as fast as she can, to leap in a perfect arc and catch it in the air, on the second bounce.

JOE FRIDAY

I waited at the curb for Jack Webb to pass on his bicycle. It was a hot day, he was serious, concentrated on the road ahead and getting wherever he was needed to be. Towards evening, I saw him again, riding the other way, coming back home I suppose. As far as I can discern, the only thing he picked up along the way was a sunburn.

WAVES

I paid for a castle with hard-earned sand dollars. It cost all I had, but now I have this unbelievable view of the ocean. I watch every moment as the tide climbs. The outer walls will stand for as long as they can, until the water pours in and flows around the castle, until it begins to tip. I know the end is coming…that's why I hold on to every precious second I can.

SEDIMENT

.

This town is still small enough that I know the delivery driver. He often shows up at work, dragging boxes the size of coffins. Then he stops to talk. I once listened to a twenty-minute story on sediment. Today, I was ambushed in my own driveway when his truck appeared. I got a cardboard carton and a ten-minute sermon about life insurance.

TIN CAN SLEEP INTERRUPTION

This morning is garbage day. Deep in the night, on the highway past our backyard, machines are banging away at I-5, opening a way for salmon to swim under the road. The wind always blows on garbage day. At 4 AM, we had to close the window. A tin can kept rattling back and forth beside the curb. If anyone would appreciate that sound, it would be John Cage. He would be lying down in the grass, making a field recording, capturing it on a spool of tape labeled "Tin Can Sleep Interruption."

The BEATLES LOVE SONGS

I lived on the seventh floor or so. My window was open and it was a warm summertime night long ago. It was almost like being in a fishbowl the way the air was dark and humid and filtered with the soft green light of the parking lot. Across the air from me someone was playing a Beatles record. One after the other, each song drifted its way to me like warm laundry drawn on a line to the moon.

The MEMORY of DEER

It's getting rare to see the deer in town. One day the memory of deer will be like those ancient Zen poems about the gibbons howling around the forest temple. Everything changes. When the deer are gone, their souls will drift into ours. You'll see more and more people feeling like deer.

THRIFTSTORE MADONNA

We do the best we can to get by. We are drawn here to beat the cost of living. Everyone comes in here looking for something. I came looking for her.

ASLEEP

Sunshine hasn't reached down deep into the weeds yet. This spot is still in shadows, the grass is wet from overnight. A blade of grass bends like a hammock where a centipede sleeps in a curl.

MUSIC for PHOTOGRAPHS

The same way you used to see trolleys, there used to be a Fotomat off Lincoln Street. One time they developed a roll of my film. I parked at the next corner and opened the envelope. As I looked through the pictures, the music began to play. It wasn't my music, these weren't my pictures, whoever took them was on some vacation in some place I'll never know.

BRIGHT WALTZING COLORS

It wasn't that strange to find a person like him, blending into the environment like a chameleon. He was on the way to work. He stood against a concrete wall waiting for the bus. He went this way every day, gliding along the cement and sidewalk effortlessly, past checkpoints and sandbags. When the flower shop blew up next to him, he was covered in bright waltzing colors.

The SEA and a SALMONBERRY

Imagine what it took for this orange berry to grow up here above the trail, like a sun on a branch near the pond. I caught it and popped it into my mouth and could taste the sweetness and the little seeds that crackled between my teeth. I thought of rapids, the sea and a salmonberry that fought its way to me.

RETIRED NAVY

When I was ten, the lady across the street brought me a cardboard box. It was filled with plastic ships. There were destroyers and a DC-3 and the USS Missouri. She explained she was cleaning her son's room and they had to go. I knew the white walls of that room, the shelves stacked with model cars and planes and even a working guillotine with a head that popped off under the falling blade. From back on their lawn, no shoes on, I saw her son staring at me. That's the way it is in war, there's always a horizon for someone where things go wrong.

DEBONAIRE

When she told me she was going to the salon to get her hair cut, I imagined her there, sitting in the chair, and what she would be saying, what the radio would be playing, how she would hold her hands. I don't know, I thought she always looked fine, I wouldn't have changed a thing about her. Oh, I was a fool in those days, I don't even think I complimented her hair. Cary Grant died two years before that happened and he never taught me how to be debonaire.

PAGE 52

Walking along the Fuji riverbank, Basho found a baby. He gave it what food he had, then he carried on. It's hard to believe he could leave it crying there. I don't know if it haunted him, but 300 years later it's still there, abandoned on page 52 of his famous journey to the North Country.

The LOST CAT

Think of all the lives that come and go on this planet.
One of them was a kitten that found me in the night.
Of course I picked it up and held it in my arms, but
I didn't feel I could hold it forever. I was just as alone
without a home and having a cat along seemed like
more than I could handle then. California made stars
overhead and I walked around in the dark asking
people I met if they lost a cat.

CATCHING the WIND

She got back to the house in the rain. She took off her black fur coat and sat on the couch next to the dog. Her hands were still cold, the dog had a warm, bristly black and white hide. I remember the way she laughed and how she took a breath before she began. Before the concert, she went into the alley and met Donovan. She had those Beatlemania eyes as she told her story.

The BEGINNING of a LONG CUP of COFFEE

I knew about the coffee shop around the corner from the bookstore. The alley brick wall was overgrown with ivy and a neon sign blazed in the leaves. It was only a street from the university. You could hear philosophy majors and historical debates. They had tablecloths. It was her choice to meet there. I didn't know much about coffee at that point, I was fine with the crystals in a jar. She wore a black and white striped shirt and red lipstick, black hair that shined in the light.

MEDICINE

I had a real knack for finding those buried blue bottles, anytime I went digging in creeks, making dams, channels, or pools. I knew they were old. Out poured sand and a trickle of muddy water. A memory of medicine. A fleck or two of gold. But I was always hoping for a rolled-up note from Billy the Kid.

The MATTRESS KING

His truck braked onto the shoulder and he asked his
son to get out with him. He found all kinds of treasure
along the road, good things thrown out for no reason
he could figure: lamps, TV sets, desks, chairs, all sorts
of slightly mistreated furniture. He liked the looks of
the mattress. Not bad, no stains. When he pressed his
hand on it, it still had some spring. He told his son to
lay down on it and close his eyes and see if he could
dream.

BOUND for SHADY GROVE

The Junebug knew it was time to retire. It took one last flight around the yard in the moonlight. Its chipped green wings beat like a cracked muffler. Then it was July. Off it went with no fanfare, down the road to Shady Grove, where it got a room next door to a fleecy Mayfly.

STARSTRUCK

The Great Great Granddaughter of Lillian Gish seemed surprised I was so happy to meet her. For me, hardly a day goes by when I'm not thinking about Chaplin and Keaton and the silent movie world. So I felt a little starstruck to meet her. I wanted to know more about her family and hear her stories. I couldn't wait to see her again. I thought of Lillian Gish in *The Wind* and *Night of the Hunter*. I felt a beam of light coming from a hundred years away.

The HERMIT of VOLTAIRE SQUARE

It was easy to close the door, draw the curtains and sit in the light of a TV. The apartment was a dreamworld there was no reason to leave. She used to sleepwalk when she was a girl, now she was where she wanted to be. Twice a week a car would deliver groceries. When she got a craving, she ordered takeout Chinese.

A BOX of PEACHES

Instead of money, the economy is counted in peaches. Today we are rich in them. We each have one, then I put the rest in a safe behind the painting of Wallace Stevens.

The ROBOT TREE on CEDAR STREET

For the moment it's on Cedar Street. It moves when it wants to, wearing tin around it like a knight clanking into battle. There's a string of red glowing cherries in its branches. I'm tempted to take one. I could bring it home and use it for a nightlight.

DIAL SET for 1872

They left their old washing machine on the lawn by
the sidewalk. It's been there for a couple days. I think
they're hoping it will disappear on its own like a time
machine popping out of sight.

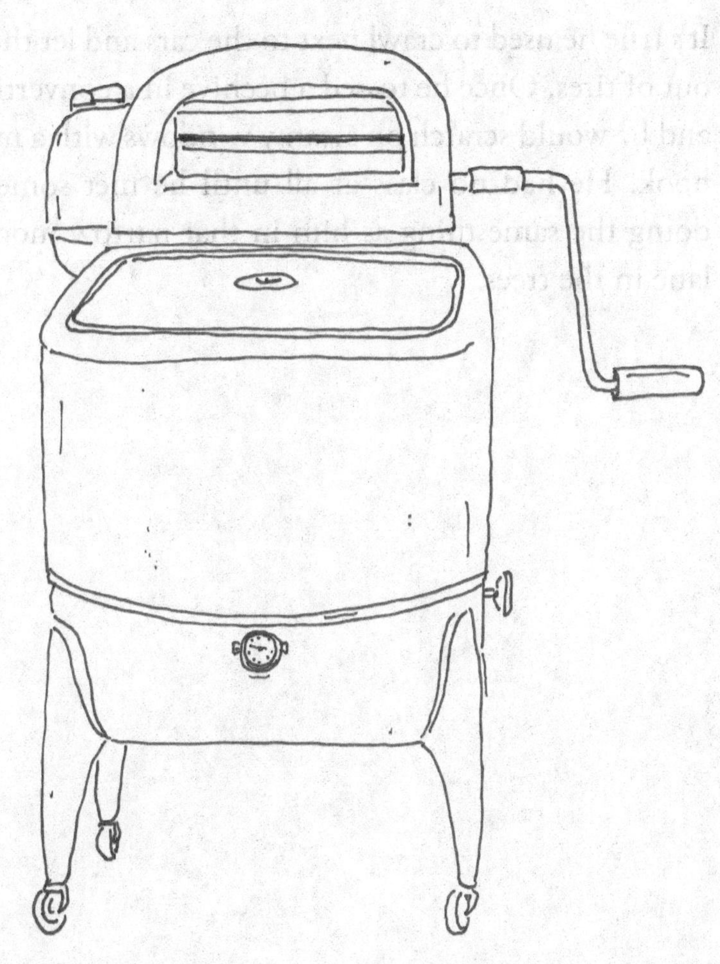

The MEANEST KID on LOVER'S LANE

It's true he used to crawl next to the cars and let the air out of tires. Once he tossed a beehive in a convertible, and he would scratch on steamy windows with a metal hook. He had no class at all until he met someone doing the same thing as him in that narrow moonlit lane in the trees.

The TIGER HUNTER

Every summer my grandparents had a garden that turned into a jungle. I helped do a little weeding and harvesting, but mostly I was responsible for locating tigers. I would look anywhere the milkweed crept in among the sweet-peas, corn and chard. They like to pounce from those tall green stalks. I had a jar stuffed with leaves and when I found a striped black and yellow caterpillar, I had to be quick to catch it before it leaped.

LAUNDROMAT ELEGY #1

I have been easily enchanted by laundromats. Even in small towns where nothing seems to be going on, people will gather in plastic chairs to watch the water do its work. They grow calm, surrounded by rows of churning washers and dryers that steam like flowers. A radio usually plays. The room is busy with coming and going like a bus station, where everyone is waiting to hold the warm familiar outlines of clothes.

LAUNDROMAT ELEGY #2

She was already a ghost, with her long white hair and pale moon-colored clothes. Behind a counter, she sat on a stool and smoked a cigarette. If a machine wasn't working right, she would move silently, open it and take a look. We spent a month or two going there before we bought our own washer and dryer. It was just easier to. We didn't go there anymore and one day the laundromat was gone. The windows were boarded over. She weaved everything inside into water and soap, and poured with that river to wherever it flowed.

The COUNTERFEIT PEACH

There's always someone willing to open Frankenstein
doors to unspeakable fate, like the counterfeit peach.
In a garage, dulled by soundproof walls, a racket of
spindles and levers, rollers, platen, treadle, a flywheel
that creaks round and round, each fruit is manufactured
and held up to a magnified eye. They're good enough
to trick the man at the newsstand, or the waitress tired
on her feet. For a little while. Oh, but it can't last. It's
an old story with a moral too: there's no way to copy a
peach, that's a miracle only nature can create.

The MAN WHO CARED for TIME

I was marooned on a couch waiting for my daughter's appointment to be done. The wall clock didn't work. The kid at the desk said it was out of batteries and returned to his computer. He wasn't concerned about time. He's not the one stuck watching the clock.

The GARAGE SALE

At a garage sale on South Hill, I saw a deer. A price tag was tied to it. I couldn't read it though. The deer kept moving around the record player, behind the wading pool and a lamp. For a moment I wondered how it would do in our yard, but I bought a toaster instead.

SEDIMENT RETURNS

I keep seeing his delivery truck driving around town. Of course, I swerve away madly out of his way, across lawns and sidewalks, knocking over garbage cans, breaking through a fence, and running over a swing-set until I can safely get to the next street.

An IMPORTANT DECISION

This is the third day the washing machine has been on our neighbor's lawn. This morning, a red truck stopped and someone crossed the road. He looked like a guy who spent his days looking for deals. He read the note taped to it: *The Spin Cycle doesn't work.* Then he went back to his truck, slammed the door and drove off.

The USED DREAM LOT

I spent last night there, back and forth, examining dreams that have been around for years. All the usual ones with dents and dings and faltering paint. I was caught until I chose, hounded by a man in a plaid suit who promised he had the perfect dream for me at a price I couldn't find anywhere else.

LEMON PROMENADE

You have to be in the right frame of mind, you have to be calm. Open the window and listen, past the jangle of the windchimes hooked to the eaves, the birds, a car alarm, through all the everyday noise, and you will know they're coming. Marching together in a wobbling roll, down the hill from the sun.

VIDEO

He was older than us by a few years and we would climb the stairs to visit his crowded apartment. He let us play records and read his books and he would listen to us, tuned into our words. My friend was afraid of becoming him. The videos, the stairs lined with newspaper stacks and brown glass bottles you had to step around.

MONA

Someone named Mona is dead in the woods. I noticed the gravestone, a scrap of cedar with her name painted on.

A FISH OUT of WATER

We've been watching her for a year as she walks past our house. I could describe the way she walks. For a while I had a nickname for her but that stopped once we started to say hello when we met. During the heatwave I told her to stay cool. This evening she stopped to pet our dog who made a royal fool of herself, jumping and wiggling like a fish out of water.

The SPLENDID PUPPET

We are delighted, impressed, we cheer and applaud. But really there's someone else, unseen, in control of all things. She put everything in a steamer trunk at the end of the show and carried it to a little hatchback car. As she balanced the trunk on the bumper, it slipped from her hands and smacked on the pavement. It might have hit her toe. She cursed and hopped and a few kids still hanging around laughed. They thought it was part of the act, as if her strings were being pulled.

FUJI'S FIVE & DIME PRIMER

This was my introduction to Japan. A store I would go to buy candy and look at robot toys. Fish-shaped flags. Statues of Buddha. Without even knowing about Mount Fuji yet, I spent sunny clear days seeing Mount Rainier on the other side of our backyard fence.

A breezy morning, cloudy too, at the top of a tree there's a bird flying a kite.

GOOD MORNING, JOHNSON DRACULA

Sleep is turning into alarm clocks all down the street. The sun has arrived and the night has crawled in with him, purring like a black cat. He rests in the basement in a casket seasoned with dirt from Transylvania. When he wakes at midnight, he carefully brushes his tuxedo clean. He's never seen the morning, but he imagines this is what it's like to face another day at the job.

The BLUE ECONOLINE

Rust has found the right address, an old van by the
side of the fence.

CHIMNEYS

When the tide was out, they were easy to find. The water washed them around and spread them like broken rooftiles. Carry the best ones back to the house, set them on the windowsills. Playing cards on the porch at night, using the shells for ashtrays.

The MOVIE STARS of HER TIME

Thinking about her final year, the movie stars of her time, I doubt Barbara Stanwyck had a room in this sort of hall. Her door is taped with a picture of flowers cut from a greeting card.

The WIND PEDDLER

The wind keeps opening the door and looking in,
searching for something, disturbing the curtains and
the dog on the floor who opens one sleeping eye.

PARIS

Mostly I remember cobblestones, the cars, Citroens, and while I was all alone I went to a bakery and got bread and cheese and found a park. I was tired. A man across from me was crying on his bench and like you would only see in a movie, a beautiful woman stopped to comfort him.

The RABBITS

I woke up early and looked out the window and
wouldn't you know, a rabbit was out there on the lawn.
I don't know what they do. Do they have a lifestyle?
So much is hidden between the times I see them. For
all I know they're directing everything.

The SILENT DISGUISE

The woods are quiet this morning. Usually the birds are singing for us. Even the creek is holding its breath. I wonder if there's a hawk nearby, or some other predator. Then a man rounds the bend pushing a bicycle. He is slow, it takes some effort for him to speak, his hands are knotted to the handlebars. I know it happens in stories—he could be a coyote in disguise, I wouldn't be surprised—that would explain the silence.

SHAMBLES

Going for our walk, I left Laurel and Hardy alone in the house. They sat at the table by the window. Calm as can be. I shut the door and we hurry. As much as I like them, I just know they'll get into trouble. They only need a few minutes to turn our house into a shambles.

The INFLATABLE POOL

This afternoon, it gets so warm the rabbits open the
doors on the lawn and stand around their tunnels
with their feet in the shallow inflatable pool.

STEAMBOAT SERVICE

Some people go to sea, I spent five years seeing the world from a dishwashing machine. Those nights we would sail into port and I was mopping the floor around the tables and the last load was clanking in the kitchen like a steamboat.

BOOTLEG OASIS

Blankets unrolled on the sidewalk, they would be selling sunglasses, gold watches, bootleg cassette tapes, necklaces and diamond rings, ready to run the second the police came. Once I saw it happen. They folded up everything and shot into the alley. Nothing but cement where there used to be an oasis.

PARKING LOT POLKA

Cars are all around him and people are walking in and out of the grocery store. The cardboard sign says, *I Found My Job*. He is elated, you can hear it in the music. What a joy he's not bewildered anymore, this is his calling. Oh, how could it have taken so long for the world to know? Every parking lot needs an accordion player.

The GINGERBREAD DOG

The way she lies in the yellow field, watching like a
lion, her fur blending in, crumbled, flopped hot out
of the oven, swept by the bristles of a weedy broom.

The WATERY BLUE GIANT

A crab holds to the rock as each new wave tries to knock it off. The ocean is a never ending current, but it's not letting go. When you live in the sea, you get used to it, the minnows and the weeds all do, moved in the breathing of the watery blue giant.

The WRONG WORD

In the 6th Grade, I got my first lesson in poetry. Our teacher had been on a gunboat in Vietnam and part of him was still there. All it took was the wrong word to set him off.

The RIGHT BIRD

She needs to step on the dappled light and touch every tree like a friend. It's not something she can keep to herself. Now I find myself doing it too. The moss on the alder, the glow in the leaves. And when we hear a bird that sounds like a parakeet, we both stop to listen.

DREAMLAND

What are they doing in Dreamland? I can see a street with palm trees, hear the motorbikes and someone sits at a table with a teacup, writing a postcard. I can't quite read the words. I'm caught in the wings of a

NEIGHBORLY

Sunflower likes to lean over the fence on green elbows, nodding with the breeze, unfazed by the honeybees, with a good view of the backyard, offering neighborly advice on the state of our home repairs, lawn care, and the summer weather in general.

CONTEMPLATING

The one cloud in the blue sky is actually a goldfish. A girl with a crayon drew it that way. When she held the piece of paper up, the fish floated off. It paddles in the air above the cottonwood trees, contemplating, wary of the steeple and telephone wires.

OUTER SPACE EMPLOYMENT AGENCY

Sun Ra and his Arkestra played downstairs, in the earth under Seattle. I didn't have a ticket, not on a dishwasher's wage, but the locked door had a window. Not much more than a porthole. The stage levitated with horns and electric glowing uniforms orbiting around the piano directing sound like the roots of flowers growing through the ceiling, the ground, up, up, upwards, bursting from the city skin into the streetlights, castaways, the late-night flickering of the rockets on Market Street.

The PETER SELLERS REPORT

Why would we be talking about a school report forty years later with the sun shining on Alder Street and a view of the bay full of sailboats? It's fun to think of comic calamities when you're walking with a friend. South Hill has some big, elegant homes from a time when they made them that way and a camera could glide along the curb and stop at a well-tended garden where a well-dressed old man in his last movie is smiling at the leaves and flowers.

CHESHIRE CAT in TRAINING

When they're just beginning, it takes effort to balance. A branch seems awful high in the air and it's not just sitting they need to do. This one was only a kitten and it faded in and out with every tentative step. A smile was something it could only manage when the job was done.

The FOGHORN GOES SIGHTSEEING

Because it doesn't get much use during the summer, not since April as far as I can remember, we went to the shore and got the foghorn. It sat on the backseat and watched the places on land it never goes. Sometimes it made a low moan, but it kept its rumble under control until we got to the ice cream parlor. Then it couldn't help itself.

CROW SHADOW

Our son's friend rides his bike to our house as dusk is falling. It's been a long hot day. There's been no rain in months. He noticed the crows on the telephone pole have their beaks open, panting. If this weather goes on much longer, one might flap down and tap on the window. A shadow asks for a glass of water.

The FAKE DOG

We were at the park when I saw the fake dog. At least that's what I told the kids. I pointed out the odd way it ran. They weren't sure. It was obvious to me anyway there was a person inside. Finally, I had to know for certain. I crossed the playing field. Big footprints have flattened the clover, but the fake dog was done running. It was sitting on a bench reading the newspaper.

SUSPENSE THEATRE

Our neighbor stands at the curb holding a piece of paper in his right hand. He looks down the street and checks his watch three times in a row, shuffling back and forth on the sidewalk. A few cars pass. If something doesn't happen soon, he's going to go back inside and shut the door and we might never know what he was waiting for.

SOMEDAY SHE'LL HAVE TO STOP
WHERE SHE CAN UNSPIN

Wherever she goes, the telltale heart of her shifting gears, she nearly drives off the road with memories.

The WIZARD of MENLO PARK

Thomas Edison would be baffled by this day and age.
He would stand in the yard. He wouldn't even be able
to open the door.

CHAPLIN AIRLINES

That was the first thing everyone asked, and yes, it was true. He was Charlie Chaplin's brother. If they wanted more, he would tell them his brother wanted to be in pictures, while he wanted to fly. These were the days you had to hold on to the pitching fuselage, riding on a bird made of cloth and wood. There's no way to describe the feeling of being in the sky. Leaving the land, the ocean below, steering for the bright sun surrounding Catalina Island.

A THANK YOU CARD

The dayshift is done, I take my dishwashing tip money and go looking for music for tonight. It isn't hard to find, it's everywhere. Since I met you, I swim in it. In the breeze with the trees and sparrows, the flowers of Salmon Street where I stop to pet a cat, a sun warmed blackberry kept rolling on my palm, each handpicked sound of this river town is caught on wax. It's all on round vinyl, thirty minutes to a side. The record player is next to the bed, we can play this tonight like a thank you card, filling the room with love and sleeping beauty.

TOPEKA FLYING BEDS

The flying beds are guided carefully across the night skies by radar. The people dreaming on them are going all over the world. Lights rushing back and forth in the stars. During the daytime, there isn't as much traffic. Mostly babies in cribs and old men lucky enough to crawl under a blanket in the middle of the day.

TOURISTS

Each weekend, we dress the part, and explore the
town as tourists. We point at things and take a lot
of pictures and we like to ask directions. We pretend
astonishment by things we've seen for years. Pretty
soon we're going further, to places we've never been.
With all our practice, we will know how to act.

FORBIBBEN PLANET

Despite the name, it has its attractions. First there are the colors and the postcard views. A robot, a futuristic house, a factory job underground. There's also a pretty girl. Unfortunately, there's a monster that creeps around unseen, killing the crew. I guess that's where the planet gets its name.

UP A LAZY RIVER

If there was a breeze, a kite could fly through the river in the air and fall down soaking, wet as a fish. The current flows overhead, rustling the dry leaves of the treetop, just out of reach. It only needs to be called, pet, coaxed to the ground and turned into rainwater.

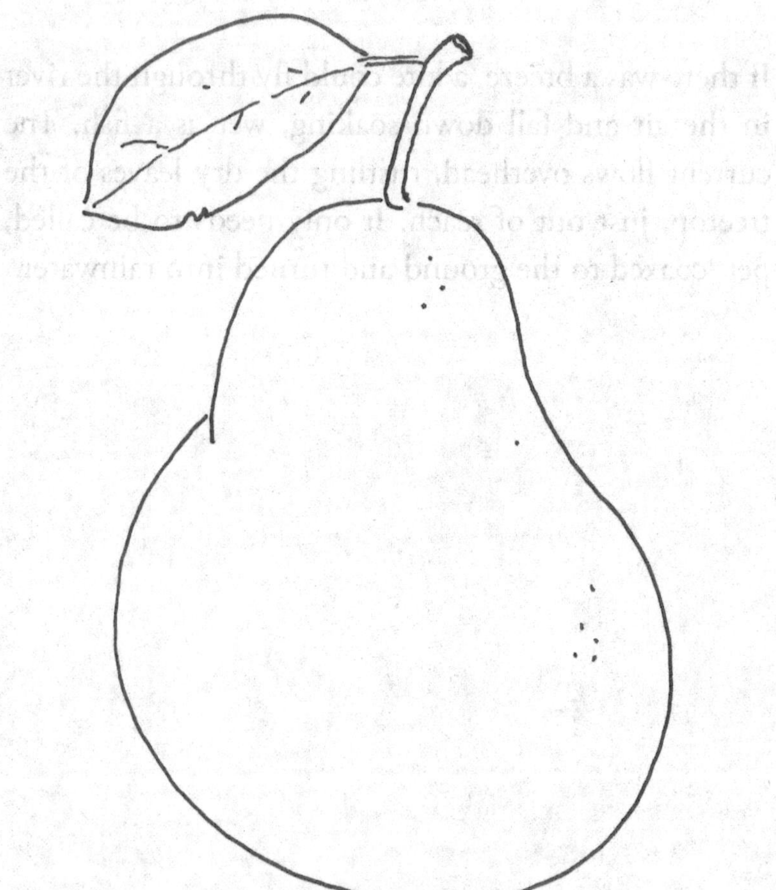

BACKSEAT PEAR

It wobbles and rolls, especially at that turn onto
Fielding Avenue where it thumped against the door.
By now we don't listen to the pear, its sense of direction
was never very good to begin with.

The SUMMER RADIO

With his back to the yellow painted house, he becomes the summer radio. A blackbird and windchimes are illustrating his slowly building story. On the other side of America, we are eagerly waiting for the words to reach us. My friend tells me, "I'm going to listen to him while pruning the suckers around my plum trees."

A HORSE NAMED CARL SANDBURG

An old white horse is riding the elevator of the Leopold. Nobody knows how it ended up in there. The crowd in the lobby watches the arrow as it rises between the floors. For a moment it rests on the 11th floor, then it's moving two stories down, then somewhere else again. By night the people have gone, except for the clerk at the desk who has grown used to it.

SPARROWS

Early on a California morning, she is holding a watering can, reaching above her head to the flower basket. There are two of them. When one is full, she tends the other. The water drains through and rains on the dry cement sidewalk. Some silver pools have formed. As soon as she goes back in the café, the sparrows appear.

The PAINTED HEART

I drove uphill on 50th next to the zoo, this was years ago. Below one of the underpasses, a girl was painting the cement wall. Gigantic bright flowers and stars and animals. I didn't know a heart could jump like that, suddenly all I wanted to do was fall in love with her and color the world with her if only I could stop the car and get out.

A FIRST-RATE FOOL

Once I read some stories on Eastlake Avenue. Like a first-rate fool, I thought up a great gag that was sure to wow the crowd. A pair of glasses with no lenses. Without knowing it, I went through the same routine as a 1936 comedy. Only no one was laughing. Anyway, I tried. I have enjoyed my time here among you and I have done my best to entertain you.

PRAYER

Oh, how we wait for an answer, as if the crooked aerial
on the roof overhead can catch your voice, as if, if not
that, the wind will deliver your message to me served
in an old-fashioned way.

TRANSPARENT APPLES

They grow on glass branches on trees that almost aren't there. You could bump into one if you're not careful. Sometimes all you see is the shadow of a tree. You'll need to hold out your arms like a sleepwalker, feel for the switch and turn the tree on like a chandelier, making every ripe apple glow.

The AIR-RAID WARDEN

When I was twelve, I was the local air-raid warden. I wore a white metal helmet from the surplus store and watched the sky as if our lives depended on it. I saw imaginary bombers and fighter planes and ran across the grass to tell everyone.

The CITY OF PHANTOMS

What happened to the people who were here? Our house was built in 1937 and I have not met the ghost of the old woman who lived here, though sometimes there's a sound in the kitchen I can't explain. Something falls off a shelf. I turn and look. Wherever she is, wherever she's gone, maybe she visits now and then in a dream.

FALLOUT SHELTER

We saw that yellow sign on the building and knew if there was a war, we could take shelter there. Even so, it was hard to believe that a basement room could protect us…that we could hold each other while the city thumped and blew away…and then, after another day, go up the stairs into a calm world that had been refreshed.

The OWL and

The pea-green boat in the light of the moon came sailing, finally sailing back home. The honey and money were long since gone, no more dancing in the tidal zone. The stars still shine the same old way, the sail is gently blown, but although the boat was built for two, the owl is all alone.

SUNDAY EVENING SUNRISE

The sun fell below the horizon. Then, pulling against all natural laws, it returned for a moment just to see you again.

The DREAM MACHINE

I don't mind walking in on movies. The television is used to me. One morning William Powell is boarding a ship. He's halfway across a black and white sea when I leave for a while to do something in reality. It's alright. This happens all the time. There's always another movie waiting. I go back and forth in dreams.

The DISCOUNT DETECTIVE

The woman in the field is looking for her lost keys.
I haven't seen them. I tell her I'll be on the lookout.
The wild grass is dry as papyrus and crumpled flat,
bigger than a parking lot. She wanders off the path.
She knows her chances are slim. Then she lights a
cigarette, smoking in the middle of a tinderbox.

THRIFTSTORE BELLS

The butterfly on the back of the door rings as I go in. There are more of them too, on the ceiling fans, clothes racks, on sale tags, on the shelves and the wingback chairs. They all have little bells they wear to let her know I'm here.

RECURRING BIRD

On Telegraph Road at the end of the day, the sidewalk sparrows line her way. They chatter and watch from the leaves. To live among us in poverty, to speak in parables and poetry, to reach out with a healing touch. She is our recurring bird. Her song is no secret, it's something we turn over and over like a prayer. In dark times we remember she is here. To stay in someone's heart is immortality.

The VIOLIN TRUCK

Since school let out two months ago, we've been missing the music. They sent trucks around town to restock the air with sounds of the orchestra and marching band. John Philip Sousa crept in the duct at an ice cream shop. The last movement of Beethoven's 8th quartet circles the corner of Maple Street like a cat. Music only stays in the air for so long. I haven't heard our son play his violin since June. I hope it happens soon. I tap the steering wheel restlessly. Our car was stopped at a traffic light behind a truck full of Bach.

THRIFTSTORE ELVIS

In a crowd of porcelain and plastic and a tin cake pan, there he is. Or his name anyway. Written in gold on a chipped coffee cup. You can also find him in the records and paperbacks. Everything has a story, how it was used for a while, served its time, and ended up with Elvis. America took him over and spun him until he was dizzy and forgot. It's a familiar song. Others arrive every day in a paper bag or box. They don't cost much. For 75 cents you can hold him and have coffee with the king.

The GOOD LITTLE BEAST

Most of the time she's fine, but on a hot day like this she can't help herself. She pulls free of the leash and dives over the bank. A splash, the water striders scatter, the overhanging berries thrash and bounce. She smiles, in deep, and stares at me out of reach. Thanks to a creek, the good little beast becomes a crocodile.

The BALSA WOOD ARMY

The balsa wood army has not lost the war. They want to assure us. Yesterday they sent 14,000 matchsticks to the front. Tomorrow the news will be printed on tissue. We should expect victory before too long.

In PRAISE of the RHINOCEROS

It stands in the shadows, squinting. The plates on its hide shiver. I'm sure it would like to be elsewhere. Whoever heard of a rhino in the woods behind the latest housing development?

The WEDDING

All over the world they're happening. Two people find each other. Whatever happens next also happened before. Holding hands, they're about to take off, and they can't say exactly where to.

The HIDDEN WORLD

We used to climb downhill through the underbrush to a mystery I still wonder about. The poison ivy had to be avoided. The slippery ground could roll you down to the shore. My cousin wore his camouflage all the time then and we were probably carrying toy guns. The narrow cavern entrance was surrounded by square cut tumbled stones. The hornets never let us get any closer.

With PLASTIC CHAIRS

I found a photo of him. A few actually. I didn't recognize any of the people around him. These were his last days. His life had been hard and the mistakes he made led him to a room with plastic chairs. He was smiling though. He's been dead for a while, but he is happy.

The BLACKBERRY TRAWLER

Hear the creak of it keeling in the field, a big dark looming made of blackberry vines, each long shoot carefully configured and welded thorn by thorn to resemble a ship. All around the base, the berries have been picked by the shipyard crew, the way they glean a hull of barnacles. The only ones left are hanging from the deck in green nets only a ladder can get to.

ADVICE from a YAK

I went to the zoo in order to see a yak specifically. I found it standing in the shade of a wall. It was 81 degrees in the sun. The poor thing looked pretty miserable. And most disappointing of all, it wasn't talking. I was turning to go when I read the graffiti on the rail, "For a good time, call Barbara."

PRESENTING MR. TABLECLOTH

He creeps from table to table, dressed in a checkered suit that matches the tablecloth. You won't see him, but you'll know he's been and gone. You may be leaning, looking into your date's lovely eyes, and the next time you reach for a buttered roll, the basket is empty.

OUT of a CLEAR BLUE SKY

After what seems like a long time, I'm seeing pregnant women again. I always get a little entranced, as if, out of a clear blue sky, a miracle will happen. A balloon will land in the backyard and when she steps from the basket, she's carrying a baby.

WHEN the EVERLY BROTHERS WERE YOUNG

The Everly brothers are still working, it's late, they need one more sale to meet quota. They park their 1945 Chevrolet in the begonias and follow the brick pathway. A porch light is on. One of these days they'll be on the radio and they can put this behind them.

LOW FLYING DRAGONFLY

Look out, it's returning, sweeping jaggedly and watching through goggles as the land below tumbles like a mighty crop, thistle deep enough to get lost in forever.

The orange cat sat across from me. "I promise…" he said and raised a paw sincerely, "I won't eat no more birds or rabbits." The ashtray next to him was overflowing. It had been a long confession. "Rats and mice are okay though," I repeated. He said, "Sure…" then his yellow eyes darted to the window, "Can I go now?" I shrugged. I had done my best. Out on the street the neon lights were beckoning.

DEAR FIONA

You wouldn't believe the outrageous letter he wrote her. It was terrible being a pirate, it didn't suit him at all. The eye patch made him dizzy. He was unprepared for the long days and nights at sea and his rowdy bad company. If only he had the courage to stay with her, before the wind carried him so far from shore. There was nothing ahead of him but more water and despair. What were the chances of his message in a bottle ever reaching her?

TWO GIANTS

There are two giants over on Mill Avenue. They tower above the trees. Their shadows fall across the roofs. Someone's dog is barking, seagulls circle around them. When they're done talking, they step over the telephone wires, not wanting to be a nuisance.

The ISLAND

After he bought the island, he had to find somewhere to put it. The park service said absolutely not, their coveted rivers and lakes were already spoken for. He couldn't just drop it in the harbor either, it would disturb the flow of shipping. Finally, he had to tow it out to sea and let it go.

The WOODPECKER

The woodpecker makes holes in the dead tree until it resembled an apartment building with empty windows letting in the summer breeze. On the 38th floor, a weevil is listening to the radio, ironing a dress made from a daisy petal. "Won't I look nice in this?" she thinks. There's a knock at her door. In her excitement she forgets about the woodpecker.

The UNHEARD BIRD

Between *The Wizard of Oz* and the end of the war, Judy Garland made sixteen movies. So did her shadow. It did everything she did, except sing. Or maybe it did. Maybe her shadow was like an unheard bird or a mermaid a mile deep. With the right kind of machines gleaned from top-secret submarines we can hear that song on another frequency.

BLACKBERRY ANNIVERSARY

We're past paper, copper and bronze, silk and jewelry, frankincense and myrrh. After twenty-five years and growing, we have our feet planted in the ground, we have all we need to make something sweet.

The MOTH in the AIRPORT

The plane from Chicago was late. People stared at the unmoving carrousel. A man was reading a brochure. He didn't notice the moth. It landed on his back for a moment. The man turned the page, there were more things to see in our town. The moth took off again and this time the man gave a jump and swung as it circled. It was okay, no harm done, just a little turbulence, as it descended to land.

CHASING APPLES in the FIELD

We came all this way and there's nothing for her to chase. I forgot to bring a ball. I was looking for a stick or something when there was a sound of rustling leaves. The nearest tree leans back, creaking bark, winds up, and throws an apple for her with all its might.

A WISE DECISION

The taxi cabs have been replaced by camels. A wise decision. The heat is relentless. The desert grit, fine as gold dust, gets into motors and tangles the gears. The city grinds to a halt. Meanwhile, my taxi waits outside. All a camel needs is a telephone call and a star to steer by.

FLOWERPOT

It was all too easy in spring to wear the flowerpot on her head. The leaves were verdant and the petals soaked her in perfume. But then the summer sun began to burn everything. She was chased by bees until she took shelter in a carwash where the fizzing soap bubbles never stopped.

VACATION on the ROOF

A pigeon wearing a cap and folding a map told me he was here for vacation. "Okay…" I supposed. Then he called his family over from the curb. They had suitcases, coolers, and a small portable TV. Wingfulls of things. They were chattering the way pigeons do as they made their way to the roof. I hear them at all hours babbling up there. They seem to really be enjoying their stay, having the time of their life.

THRIFTSTORE MADONNA

Written in Summer 2021

published in chronological order

(except for "Someday She'll Have To…" from 1993)

From *Pie in the Sky* #76, 1993

Books by Good Deed Rain

Saint Lemonade, Allen Frost, 2014. Two novels illustrated by the author in the manner of the old Big Little Books.

Playground, Allen Frost, 2014. Poems collected from seven years of chapbooks.

Roosevelt, Allen Frost, 2015. A Pacific Northwest novel set in July, 1942, when a boy and a girl search for a missing elephant. Illustrated throughout by Fred Sodt.

5 Novels, Allen Frost, 2015. Novels written over five years, featuring circus giants, clockwork animals, detectives and time travelers.

The Sylvan Moore Show, Allen Frost, 2015. A short story omnibus of 193 stories written over 30 years.

Town in a Cloud, Allen Frost, 2015. A three part book of poetry, written during the Bellingham rainy seasons of fall, winter, and spring.

A Flutter of Birds Passing Through Heaven: A Tribute to Robert Sund, 2016. Edited by Allen Frost and Paul Piper. The story of a legendary Ish River poet & artist.

At the Edge of America, Allen Frost, 2016. Two novels in one book blend time travel in a mythical poetic America.

Lake Erie Submarine, Allen Frost, 2016. A two week vacation in Ohio inspired these poems, illustrated by the author.

and Light, Paul Piper, 2016. Poetry written over three years. Illustrated with watercolors by Penny Piper.

The Book of Ticks, Allen Frost, 2017. A giant collection of 8 mysterious adventures featuring Phil Ticks. Illustrated throughout by Aaron Gunderson.

I Can Only Imagine, Allen Frost, 2017. Five adventures of love and heartbreak dreamed in an imaginary world. Cover & color illustrations by Annabelle Barrett.

The Orphanage of Abandoned Teenagers, Allen Frost, 2017. A fictional guide for teens and their parents. Illustrated by the author.

In the Valley of Mystic Light: An Oral History of the Skagit Valley Arts Scene, 2017. A comprehensive illustrated tribute. Edited by Claire Swedberg & Rita Hupy.

Different Planet, Allen Frost, 2017. Four science fiction adventures: reincarnation, robots, talking animals, outer space and clones. Cover & illustrations by Laura Vasyutynska.

Go with the Flow: A Tribute to Clyde Sanborn, 2018. Edited by Allen Frost. The life and art of a timeless river poet. In beautiful living color!

Homeless Sutra, Allen Frost, 2018. Four stories: Sylvan Moore, a flying monk, a water salesman, and a guardian rabbit.

The Lake Walker, Allen Frost 2018. A little novel set in black and white like one of those old European movies about death and life.

A Hundred Dreams Ago, Allen Frost, 2018. A winter book of poetry and prose. Illustrated by Aaron Gunderson.

Almost Animals, Allen Frost, 2018. A collection of linked stories, thinking about what makes us animals.

The Robotic Age, Allen Frost, 2018. A vaudeville magician and his faithful robot track down ghosts. Illustrated throughout by Aaron Gunderson.

Kennedy, Allen Frost, 2018. This sequel to *Roosevelt* is a coming-of-age fable set during two weeks in 1962 in a mythical Kennedyland. Illustrated throughout by Fred Sodt.

Fable, Allen Frost, 2018. There's something going on in this country and I can best relate it in fable: the parable of the rabbits, a bedtime story, and the diary of our trip to Ohio.

Elbows & Knees: Essays & Plays, Allen Frost, 2018. A thrilling collection of writing about some of my favorite subjects, from B-movies to Brautigan.

The Last Paper Stars, Allen Frost 2019. A trip back in time to the 20 year old mind of Frankenstein, and two other worlds of the future.

Walt Amherst is Awake, Allen Frost, 2019. The dreamlife of an office worker. Illustrated throughout by Aaron Gunderson.

When You Smile You Let in Light, Allen Frost, 2019. An atomic love story written by a 23 year old.

Pinocchio in America, Allen Frost, 2019. After 82 years buried underground, Pinocchio returns to life behind a car repair shop in America.

Taking Her Sides on Immortality, Robert Huff, 2019. The long awaited poetry collection from a local, nationally renowned master of words.

Florida, Allen Frost, 2019. Three days in Florida turned into a book of sunshine inspired stories.

Blue Anthem Wailing, Allen Frost, 2019. My first novel written in college is an apocalyptic, Old Testament race through American shadows while Amelia Earhart flies overhead.

The Welfare Office, Allen Frost, 2019. The animals go in and out of the office, leaving these stories as footprints.

Island Air, Allen Frost, 2019. A detective novel featuring haiku, a lost library book and streetsongs.

Imaginary Someone, Allen Frost, 2020. A fictional memoir featuring 45 years of inspirations and obstacles in the life of a writer.

Violet of the Silent Movies, Allen Frost, 2020. A collection of starry-eyed short story poems, illustrated by the author.

The Tin Can Telephone, Allen Frost, 2020. A childhood memory novel set in 1975 Seattle, illustrated by author like a coloring book.

Heaven Crayon, Allen Frost, 2020. How the author's first book Ohio Trio would look if printed as a Big Little Book. Illustrated by the author.

Old Salt, Allen Frost, 2020. Authors of a fake novel get chased by tigers. Illustrations by the author.

A Field of Cabbages, Allen Frost, 2020. The sequel to The Robotic Age finds our heroes in a race against time to save Sunny Jim's ghost. Illustrated by Aaron Gunderson.

River Road, Allen Frost, 2020. A paperboy delivers the news to a ghost town. Illustrated by the author.

The Puttering Marvel, Allen Frost, 2021. Eleven short stories with illustrations by the author.

Something Bright, Allen Frost, 2021. 106 short story poems walking with you from winter into spring. Illustrated by the author.

The Trillium Witch, Allen Frost, 2021. A detective novel about witches in the Pacific Northwest rain. Illustrated by the author.

Cosmonaut, Allen Frost, 2021. Yuri Gagarin stars in this novel that follows his rocket landing in an American town. Midnight jazz, folk music, mystery and sorcery. Illustrated by the author.

Thriftstore Madonna, Allen Frost, 2021. 124 summer story poems. Illustrated by the author.

Laundromat
Self Serv